KT-481-674

Lost in
the Jurassic

Cardiff Libraries
www.cardiff.gov.uk/libraries

Llyfrgelloedd Caerdyd
www.caerdydd.gov.uk/llyfrgelloe

CARDIFF
CAERDYDD

ACC. No: 07014117

Dinosaur Cove™

A Jurassic Adventure

Dinosaur Cove™

Lost in
the Jurassic

by
REX STONE

illustrated by
MIKE SPOOR

Series created by
Working Partners Ltd

OXFORD
UNIVERSITY PRESS

Special thanks to Jan Burchett and Sara Vogler

For Samuel Stephen Dyche R.S.

For Kate Adams for your creative input
during my Jurassic times M.S.

OXFORD
UNIVERSITY PRESS

Great Clarendon Street, Oxford OX2 6DP
Oxford University Press is a department of the University of Oxford.
It furthers the University's objective of excellence in research, scholarship,
and education by publishing worldwide in

Oxford   New York

Auckland   Cape Town   Dar es Salaam   Hong Kong   Karachi
Kuala Lumpur   Madrid   Melbourne   Mexico City   Nairobi
New Delhi   Shanghai   Taipei   Toronto

With offices in

Argentina   Austria   Brazil   Chile   Czech Republic   France   Greece
Guatemala   Hungary   Italy   Japan   Poland   Portugal   Singapore
South Korea   Switzerland   Thailand   Turkey   Ukraine   Vietnam

Oxford is a registered trade mark of Oxford University Press
in the UK and in certain other countries

© Working Partners Limited 2010
Illustrations © Mike Spoor 2010
Series created by Working Partners Ltd

Dinosaur Cove is a registered trademark of Working Partners Ltd

The moral rights of the author have been asserted

Database right Oxford University Press (maker)

First published 2010
First published in this edition 2014

All rights reserved. No part of this publication may be reproduced,
stored in a retrieval system, or transmitted, in any form or by any means,
without the prior permission in writing of Oxford University Press,
or as expressly permitted by law, or under terms agreed with the appropriate
reprographics rights organization. Enquiries concerning reproduction
outside the scope of the above should be sent to the Rights Department,
Oxford University Press, at the address above

You must not circulate this book in any other binding or cover
and you must impose this same condition on any acquirer

British Library Cataloguing in Publication Data

Data available

ISBN: 978-0-19-273409-9

3 5 7 9 10 8 6 4

Printed in Great Britain

Paper used in the production of this book is a natural,
recyclable product made from wood grown in sustainable forests
The manufacturing process conforms to the environmental
regulations of the country of origin

FACT FILE

➡ JAMIE'S DAD'S MUSEUM ON THE BOTTOM FLOOR OF THE LIGHTHOUSE IN DINOSAUR COVE IS THE SECOND BEST PLACE IN THE WORLD TO BE. THE FIRST IS DINO WORLD, OF COURSE, WHERE JAMIE AND HIS BEST FRIEND, TOM, CAN VISIT THE JURASSIC ERA AND SEE

REAL, LIVE DINOSAURS!

BUT THE THING ABOUT VISITING DINO WORLD IS THAT YOU'RE SUPPOSED TO BE ABLE TO COME BACK...

JAMIE

Jamie's eye

Jamie's hand

Jamie's foot

- **FULL NAME:** JAMIE MORGAN
- **AGE:** 8 YEARS
- **SIZE:** 1.3 METRES
- **TOP SPEED:** 10 KPH
- **LIKES:** FOSSIL HUNTING AND LEARNING ABOUT DINOSAURS
- **DISLIKES:** BEING STUCK INDOORS

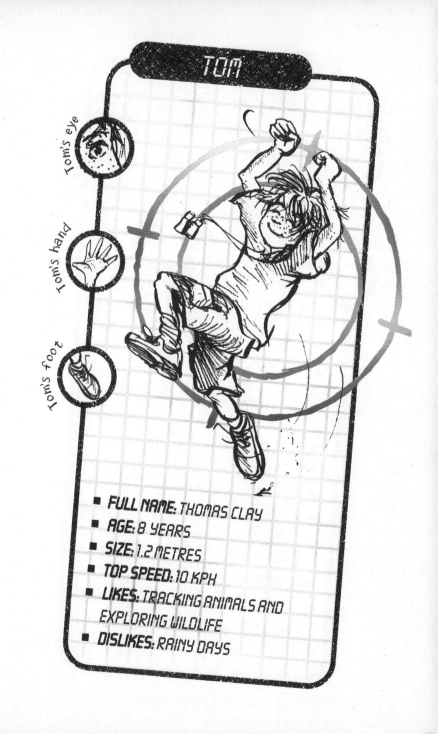

TOM

Tom's eye

Tom's hand

Tom's foot

- **FULL NAME:** THOMAS CLAY
- **AGE:** 8 YEARS
- **SIZE:** 1.2 METRES
- **TOP SPEED:** 10 KPH
- **LIKES:** TRACKING ANIMALS AND EXPLORING WILDLIFE
- **DISLIKES:** RAINY DAYS

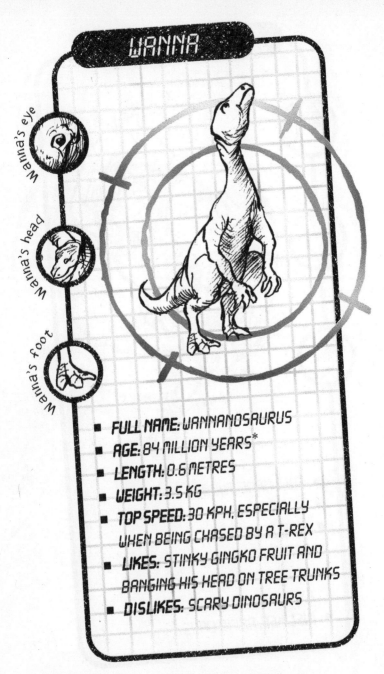

WANNA

Wanna's eye

Wanna's head

Wanna's foot

- **FULL NAME:** WANNANOSAURUS
- **AGE:** 84 MILLION YEARS*
- **LENGTH:** 0.6 METRES
- **WEIGHT:** 3.5 KG
- **TOP SPEED:** 30 KPH, ESPECIALLY WHEN BEING CHASED BY A T-REX
- **LIKES:** STINKY GINGKO FRUIT AND BANGING HIS HEAD ON TREE TRUNKS
- **DISLIKES:** SCARY DINOSAURS

*NOTE: SCIENTISTS CALL THIS PERIOD THE LATE CRETACEOUS

PTEROSAUR

Pterosaur's tail

Pterosaur's claw

Pterosaur's teeth

Pterosaur's eye

- **FULL NAME:** PTEROSAUR – MEANS WINGED LIZARD
- **AGE:** 65 – 220 MILLION YEARS*
- **LENGTH:** UP TO 17 METRES, FROM THE SIZE OF A BAT TO THE SIZE OF AN AEROPLANE
- **WEIGHT:** UP TO 6 KG
- **LIKES:** HEIGHTS
- **DISLIKES:** BIGGER PREDATORS

*NOTE: SCIENTISTS CALL THIS PERIOD THE JURASSIC

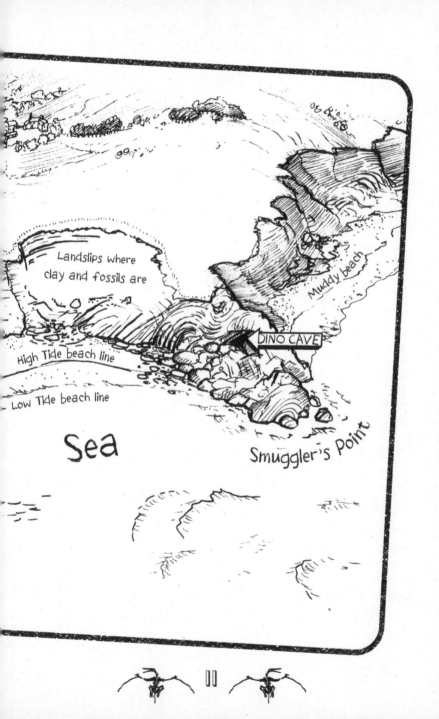

CHAPTER 1

'Check out that massive fossil!' exclaimed Jamie Morgan as he stared at the picture of the huge dinosaur bone on the poster in front of him. 'That must have been some dino!'

Jamie's dad had just put up a new display in the museum on the ground floor of their lighthouse home. It was all about the first discovery of the dinosaurs.

His best friend
Tom Clay nodded.
'This megalosaurus
thigh bone was dug

up over three hundred years ago,' he read. 'Wow! No one knew dinosaurs existed then. It says here that people thought it was the bone of an ancient giant human.'

'We know that's not true,' said Jamie. 'But wouldn't it have been cool if it was?'

Tom strode up and down between the exhibit cases, swinging his arms fiercely. 'Here comes Tom the Prehistoric Giant ready to take on all attackers.'

'He wouldn't have stood a chance against Jamie the Jurassic Megalosaur,' declared Jamie, raising his hands like claws and charging after him.

'We'll see about that!' boomed Tom in his deepest voice. 'I'll just uproot a handy tree and whack you

over the head.' He swung the pretend weapon at Jamie, who was roaring and snapping at his enemy.

'Mind my exhibits!' laughed Mr Morgan as he went by with Jamie's grandad, carrying boxes to the museum office.

Jamie took another look at the poster and lowered his voice. 'You know, our secret Dino World would be very different if humans had been around all that time ago.'

'But we like it the way it is,' replied Tom firmly. 'Just us and the dinosaurs.'

Jamie and Tom had discovered the hidden entrance to a world of living dinosaurs in the back of a secret cave. No one else knew that the two friends sneaked off to Dino World for amazing prehistoric adventures.

'Come and look at the news, boys!' Jamie's grandad called. 'You're not going to believe what this scientist has found.'

Jamie and Tom ran into the office, where his dad and grandad were gazing at the TV on the wall. Grandad handed over a bag of toffees for Jamie and Tom to snack on while they watched.

A reporter was standing outside
a cave, holding out his microphone
to a fierce looking man in a hat.

'Are you sure you haven't made
a mistake, Professor Jenkins?' the
reporter was saying.

'I'm certain,' insisted
the scientist, looking
intently at the camera.
'The world may not

be ready for this discovery but I'm telling you that human beings lived as long ago as the Jurassic era.'

Jamie and Tom gawped at the screen.

'It can't be true, can it, Dad?' Jamie asked his father, with a worried glance at Tom.

Mr Morgan laughed. 'He must have got it wrong,' he said. 'There's never been any evidence.'

'Could you show us the proof that backs up your claim?' the reporter asked the professor.

'I have it right here,' answered the professor, 'trapped millions of years ago in this piece of amber.'

He held up the transparent orange amber. The camera zoomed in on it. Embedded deep inside was a small white tooth.

'And you claim this is a human one!' said the reporter.

'Indeed it is!' replied the professor. 'We found it in Jurassic rock. Once we extract DNA from this tooth, we shall be able to prove that early humans really did live two hundred and fifty million years ago.'

Jamie's grandad shook his head.

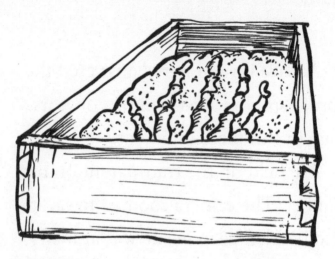

'It's all poppycock,' he muttered.

Jamie turned to his dad. 'Imagine
if it was true and you had to
reorganize the whole museum!'

'Don't even think about it!'
laughed Jamie's dad. 'I'd have to have
much more proof. Maybe someone's
put that tooth in resin as a joke.'

The scientist was now holding
a box up towards the camera.

Tom gasped. 'That doesn't look like a joke!' he exclaimed.

Lying in the box was what looked like a fossilized human hand!

The reporter stared hard into the camera. 'This is a most amazing discovery. Experts will be examining these finds this very afternoon. Tune in for an update at four o'clock.'

Mr Morgan grinned at Jamie and Tom. 'Don't look so worried, boys. We won't be turning the museum upside down yet. There'll be another explanation for those fossils.' He switched the TV off. 'If there were humans at the time of the dinosaurs scientists would have found evidence of them long before now. After all, they've been digging up dino bones for three hundred years.'

'We're going to do a bit of research on this ourselves,' said Jamie, catching Tom's eye. 'See you later.'

'Make sure you're back by four,' called Grandad. 'That reporter chappy said there'll be more news on the tooth then.'

'We will!' yelled the boys.

The boys dashed from the office.

'This is terrible!' whispered Tom when they were out of

earshot. 'What if those remains really are human? We've never seen any signs of human beings in our parts of the Jurassic.'

'I reckon Dad's right,' muttered Jamie, thinking it out. 'There can't have been people living all that time ago . . . so there's only one other explanation of the scientist's find.'

'Maybe we're not the only ones to have found a way into Dino World,' gasped Tom.

'It has been a long time since we've been to the Jurassic,' said Jamie.

'What if someone's been and everything's changed?' Tom wondered.

Jamie looked at him in horror. 'If other humans have been there . . . '

' . . . they might not keep it quiet,' finished Tom. 'Everyone would know about our secret world.'

'Tourists would come and trample all over it,' said Jamie, 'and I bet the scientists wouldn't leave it alone.'

'Come on,' said Tom. 'We've got to go to Dino World and see what's going on.'

CHAPTER 2

Jamie swung his backpack on to his shoulder and the two boys scrambled up the rough rocky path from Muddy Beach to Smuggler's Point. Once inside the dark cave high in the cliff, Jamie took out his torch and crawled through the smaller cave at the back, where a row of fossilized dinosaur footprints led to the far wall. Then he hesitated.

'What's up?' asked Tom. 'We haven't forgotten anything, have we?' Jamie shook his head. 'Compass, Fossil Finder–and I

picked
up a Jurassic
ammonite as we left,
so we'll go back to the right
time period. And I've got the toffees
Grandad gave us if we get hungry.'

'Then what are we waiting for?'
asked Tom.

'I've been thinking,' said Jamie.
'If other people have found a way
into Dino World they might have
broken the magic that takes *us* there.
We'd never be able to pass through

that wall again.' He gulped.
'We won't find out until we try,'

said Tom. 'But we must be careful.
If there are people there, they might
not want us around.'

'You're right.' Jamie nodded. 'We
mustn't be seen by anyone else.'

'I've just thought of something
even worse,' said Tom. 'If they're not
friendly, Wanna might not be safe.'

They stared at each other in the
gloomy light. Every time they went
to Dino World they met their little
wannanosaurus friend. He was
a Cretaceous dinosaur but he was a
part of the magic of Dino World and
he came on all their adventures.

'We can't let anything happen to

Wanna!' Jamie said fiercely as he placed his feet in the footprints.

Jamie usually felt a tingling rush of excitement every time he and Tom went on a new prehistoric adventure. But today was different. His stomach felt tight with anxiety. The future of Dino World might depend on them.

One . . . two . . . three . . . four . . . FIVE . . . The boys counted aloud as they stepped towards the

craggy rock wall. With a flash of light
the wall vanished. They followed the
dinosaur prints, which were now
fresh and muddy, through Gingko
Cave and out into the steaming heat
of the Jurassic world. All about them,
giant insects flew in and out among
the huge trees of the jungle.

'I know we've got a serious mission, but it's great to be back in the Jurassic,' sighed Jamie.

'And there are no fresh human footprints,' said Tom, scanning the ground. 'So no one's come in this way–at least not recently.'

'Phew,' said Jamie. 'Next we've got to make sure Wanna-OOOF!'

Something small and heavy

suddenly bowled into him, knocking
him off his feet.

Grunk! Grunk!

'Wanna!' yelled Tom. 'You're OK!'

'That's great,' puffed Jamie,
trying to stop the excited little
wannanosaurus from licking his face
completely off.

'We've got a mission, Wanna,'
Tom told him as his friend struggled
to his feet. 'Want to come with us?'

'Try and stop him.' Jamie laughed
as Wanna galloped round and round
their feet. 'Let's think—we need to
get to a good vantage point of Dino
World.'

Tom got out his compass. 'If we go north we'll be heading through the jungle,' he said.

'We could find a tall tree and look out over the plains,' suggested Jamie.

With Wanna scampering at their heels, they ploughed through the ferns and pushed aside creepers that hung between the dense trunks. After a while the little dinosaur began to nudge their legs, almost tripping them up.

'I know what you want,' said Tom.

'Gingkoes. And I think I can see
some coming up.'

SQUAARRRK!

An ear piercing sound split the air.

The boys instinctively dived behind
a rock.

'What's that?' gasped Tom, peering
out.

The leaves of the nearby trees swayed violently. The next second a group of towering dinosaurs had burst into view. The boys could see a forest of tall, stout legs stomping about, and

long necks craning to reach the gingko fruit in the branches above.

'We're lucky,' said Jamie. 'They're herbivores.'

'They're awesome,' said Tom as the gigantic bodies barged each other for the best fruit. Their young dived for anything that dropped to the ground.

Jamie whipped out his Fossil Finder. He

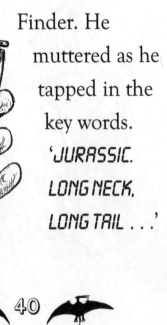

muttered as he tapped in the key words. 'JURASSIC. LONG NECK, LONG TAIL . . .'

'A single sharp claw on each foot . . . ' added Tom.

'*SMALL HEAD, BLUNT SNOUT* . . . ' In an instant, the Fossil Finder knew the answer. 'They're camarasaurs,' Jamie said.

Grunk! Grunk!

Wanna dashed in amongst the huge beasts, making a lunge for every gingko that fell to the ground. But the young cammies always got there first.

Their little friend suddenly put his head down and pawed the ground.

'Uh oh,' said Jamie. 'Wanna's going to try and shake a gingko down just like he does to the trees. He's about to ram the cammies!'

'No, Wanna!' shouted Jamie.
'You'll upset dino dinnertime.'

Wanna paused for a moment and
watched the boys curiously, but kept
looking back towards the cammies'
legs. 'We'll have to lure him away
before he causes a stampede,' Tom
said. 'And there's only one thing
that's sure to work–a personal supply
of his favourite stinky snack.'

He crept out from his hiding place
and made for an overhanging branch
laden with orange gingko fruit. He
quickly picked a handful, but as he
turned back he found himself face
to face with a baby cammie bending
down to inspect him. Tom gulped

as the baby cocked its head and
looked at him with big wide eyes.
He held out a gingko and felt the
young dinosaur's slobbery nose in
his palm as it snatched its snack
and ambled off. Tom took

his chance and dashed back to join
Jamie.

Grunk!

Wanna barged into him, pinning
him to a tree. He turned to see the
little dinosaur glaring at him.

Jamie laughed. 'Wanna came
over as soon as he saw you feeding
the cammie. He thinks all gingkoes
should be for him.'

'I'd rather feed him than a three
metre high baby dino,' said Tom.
'Here you are, Wanna. We'll take the
rest for later.'

While Wanna gobbled his snack,
Tom picked up a fallen leaf and

wrapped the rest of the smelly fruit
in it. Wanna grunked round him,
hoping for another treat.

'Give me your backpack,
Jamie,' said Tom. 'I'll
hide these in it before
our greedy little friend
gets hold of them.' Jamie
passed it to him and Tom
stowed the package inside. He grabbed
the toffees. 'Want one?' he asked.

'Oh, yes please,' replied Jamie.
'Wanna's had his treat so we can
have one too.'

Tom popped one into his mouth
and handed a couple to Jamie. 'I'll

take the backpack for a while.' He swung it on to his shoulder.

Jamie peered ahead. 'That looks a good tree to climb,' he said. 'I bet we'll be able to see for miles from the top.'

He set off, chewing as he went.

Tom and Wanna caught him up at the base of a towering gingko tree.

Jamie grinned. 'Race you to the top.'

The boys scrambled up the enormous tree. The thick, gnarly branches made easy footholds and they were soon high among the leaves. Wanna grunked anxiously as his friends disappeared from sight.

'Beat you!' declared Jamie at last. He was clinging to a swaying branch above Tom's head.

'Not fair,' laughed Tom, pulling himself up to join him. 'I had the backpack weighing me down.'

Jamie grinned. 'I still won.' He pushed aside the leaves in front of him. 'Wow! This is such a great view.'

The boys stared out in awe at
Dino World spread before them.
The dense jungle covered all the
nearby hilly land and below it the
plains stretched away until it met the
volcanic peaks in the far distance.

Tom grasped the trunk firmly with his legs and pulled his binoculars out of the backpack. He scanned the plains, from the Massive Canyon in the west right across to the sparkling river in the east.

'What's that?' said
Jamie, pointing to
a cloud of dust over
by the Humongous

Waterfall. 'Is it people?'

Tom swung his binoculars on the scene. 'It's OK,' he said in relief. 'It's just dinosaurs.'

Tom passed the binoculars to Jamie so he could see that it was an allosaurus attacking two stegosaurs. The steggies were putting up a good defence. The boys could hear the

angry roars of the huge beasts right across the plains. High in the air above the fight, a pair of pterosaurs were circling like vultures.

Tom pretended to talk to an imaginary camera. 'Tom Clay reporting from the top of a tree on an important dino mission.'

Jamie chuckled. Tom wanted to be a wildlife reporter when he grew up, and he took every chance to practise.

'An awesome allosaurus has taken on two plucky stegosaurs,' Tom went on. 'He wants his lunch–they want to stay alive. It's a fierce fight. One thing's for certain, the pterosaurs

hovering overhead are waiting to feast on whoever loses.'

The boys watched as the allosaurus clamped its jaws on the neck of one of its prey. Then it staggered back as the other stegosaurus gave it a thump with its armoured tail.

'They're evenly matched, viewers,' reported Tom. 'Hard to tell who's going to win this fight. Meanwhile, the pterosaurs have given up on their steggie lunch. They're coming this way. Looks like they're checking out the trees.'

'I'm glad Wanna's safely hidden below,' said Jamie. 'Those claws look vicious.'

'I think the allosaurus has had enough,' said Tom. 'He's making a lot of noise but he's moving away.'

'Time to get on with our search then,' said Jamie.

'Let's go,' Tom replied. 'That professor said the fossils were found in the mountains.'

'Then we should make for the Misty Mountains,' answered Jamie, 'and check out as much as we can.'

Suddenly a huge shadow fell over the boys.

'Watch out!' shouted Jamie.

CAAAW!

A sharp cry split the air and with it the beat of thick, leathery wings. One of the gigantic pterosaurs was swooping down towards Tom.

Tom yelped with terror as the huge creature's talons seized his arm in a vicelike grip and ripped him from the tree. The other pterosaur caught Tom's flailing leg in its sharp claws.

Horrified and helpless, Jamie watched as the two predators carried his friend up into the air and away over the jungle.

CHAPTER 4

Jamie scrambled down from the tree, making a huge jump to the ground in his hurry to follow the pterosaurs. The flying lizards, with their dangling catch, were now tiny dots in the distant sky. He started to sprint after them towards the Misty Mountains.

Grunk!

Wanna belted along beside him, looking around as if puzzled that Tom hadn't appeared from the gingko tree. They slashed their way through the ferns and spiky bushes. Jamie could feel his chest heaving as he sucked in air but he had to keep going.

Tom was in terrible danger. If he didn't find a way to help him, his best friend was going to be pterosaur lunch! A dreadful thought

hit him. Supposing
it was *Tom's* fossilized
hand that the scientist
had found!

'That's not going to happen,' he
panted to himself through gritted
teeth. 'I'm going to rescue him.'

Wanna suddenly stopped and
began to snuffle about in the
undergrowth. He looked up, squashed
gingko fruit pulp all over his nose.

Jamie skidded to a halt. 'There
isn't time for snacking!' he urged.
'We've got to find out where Tom's
been taken.'

Grunk!

Wanna's call sounded urgent.

'Come on, boy,' coaxed Jamie,
trying to fight down his panic. 'We've
got to go. They're getting away. You
can have some nice gingkoes later.'

But the little wannanosaurus
bounded up to him and gave him
a nudge, making Jamie stumble
downhill.

'What are you doing?'
Jamie demanded.

Wanna licked his sticky snout and pushed Jamie again. Then he darted forwards and snaffled up another smashed gingko.

Gingkoes? thought Jamie. Something wasn't right about what he was seeing but he couldn't quite pinpoint what it was.

'This isn't helping Tom,' he said out loud. 'You can stuff your face if you want, Wanna. I'm not waiting.'

Wanna didn't look up. He'd trotted on and found another squashed snack, this time under a clump of ferns.

Jamie peered up through the trees, searching desperately for a sight of the pterosaurs. And then he realized what had bothered him. He was standing amongst cycads and tall spiky conifers. There wasn't a single gingko tree to be seen in this part of the jungle. So where was Wanna finding the stinky fruits?

Then the answer came to him.

'Tom!' he yelled, punching the air. 'It has to be.'

Somehow Tom must have managed to take the gingkoes out of the backpack and drop them as he was whizzed through the air. He

Tom!

was leaving a trail for them to follow.
He'd known Wanna wouldn't be able
to resist his favourite food. Jamie felt
his spirits lifting.

'I'm sorry, boy,' he called, running
over to join his dino friend. 'You
were heading in the right direction
all along. Lead the way.'

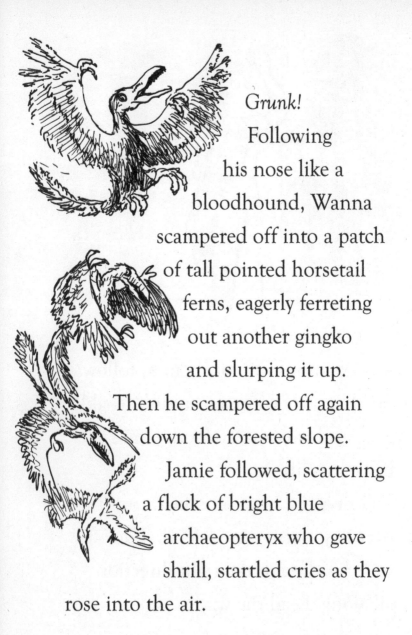

Grunk!
Following
his nose like a
bloodhound, Wanna
scampered off into a patch
of tall pointed horsetail
ferns, eagerly ferreting
out another gingko
and slurping it up.
Then he scampered off again
down the forested slope.
Jamie followed, scattering
a flock of bright blue
archaeopteryx who gave
shrill, startled cries as they
rose into the air.

Soon Jamie and Wanna had left the jungle and were out on the huge plains. A herd of diplodocuses were grazing in the distance. Even in his panic to keep chasing after Tom, Jamie couldn't help thinking how awesome they were, stretching their long necks up to the tall trees.

Wanna dashed towards yet another fruit, splattered all over a low rock.

He gulped it down and raised his
head, looking to see where his next
treat was.

'Even I saw that one,' laughed
Jamie.

He patted the eager little dinosaur
on his domed head.

'I never thought that your love
of those stinky things would come
in so useful. You'll be able to lead us
to Tom!'

CHAPTER 5

Far away, high above the plains, Tom was being sped towards the mountains. The wind buffeted his face, making his eyes stream. But much worse was the pulling and stretching of his arm and leg, clamped tightly in the pterosaurs' claws.

The land rose up now on either side. The pterosaurs made for

a narrowing valley, dragging Tom
through the top branches of the trees
that filled the steep sides. Far below
him a river raced back down towards
the swampy jungle.

I have to get my bearings, he thought
to himself as the branches scratched
and scraped at his trailing leg. *So
I can find my way back if they ever
put me down.*

The sides of the valley
were becoming steep cliffs.
'Whoah!' he cried as
the pterosaurs suddenly
plummeted in the air,
twisting and turning. His arm felt

as if it was being pulled out of
its socket. One of the flying
lizards shifted its grip and
he nearly fell. He reached up
with his other hand and clutched the
scaly leg tightly.

What was going on? Then he
heard a fierce screech and saw
another pterosaur bearing down on
them. His captors answered with
angry squawks but the rival kept on
coming. It snapped at their wings
and then at Tom.

Uh oh, he thought desperately.
*They're squabbling over who's
going to eat me.*

Whoosh!

Suddenly in front of him a sheer cliff face loomed up. The pterosaurs weren't looking where they were going. He was going to be dashed against hard rock. With a horrible wrench to his ankle, they turned away at the last second.

But this had brought them back in the path of the other flying lizard. It snapped again at Tom. He kicked out hard at the cruel beak and knocked it aside. The attacking pterosaur scrabbled desperately with its claws, catching his backpack and nearly pulling it off. Tom tugged at it. There were things inside too precious to lose.

'You're not having that!' he yelled, and yanked it free.

The pterosaur was wheeling around in the air, getting ready for another attack. But it seemed that Tom's captors weren't going

to wait for that.
They whizzed down,
straight at the cliff.
Tom could see the
rock hurtling towards
him again.

Just when he
thought he really was
going to be splattered
this time, they changed
their course and flew upwards, close
to the cliff. Then the pterosaurs let
go of him! He tumbled through the
air . . . and landed with a
thud on a hard
ledge.

He scrambled up to a sitting position and peered out. His captors were swooping after their rival, screeching loudly.

'Now where am I?' he muttered to himself.

He had been deposited on a rock shelf in the foothills of the Misty Mountains. He could see the plains and the forest beyond, a short way down the valley. Next to him was a pile of branches and leaves. He peeked into it and saw five massive eggs.

His heart sank. *This is the pterosaurs' nest and I'm definitely on the menu.*

'Not if I can help it,' he said aloud.

The first thing he had to do was complete his gingko trail. He couldn't see any sign of Jamie and Wanna but he hoped desperately they were somewhere in the trees, making their way along the valley towards him. He decided to drop another gingko right over the edge for them to find. He rummaged inside his backpack.

There was just one left. Tom watched it plummet and land *splat!* on the rocky ground far below.

SPLAT!

Now he'd done all he could to help his friends find him. He hoped it was enough. He sat on the ledge, anxiously scanning the air for the return of the pterosaurs.

CHAPTER 6

'We've almost reached the Misty Mountains,' panted Jamie as he and Wanna sprinted across the dry, dusty plains. 'Tom's got to be there somewhere.'

From the edge of the plains he scoured the tree-covered valley that led to the mountain foothills. The fast flowing river came down from it and wound away to the east.

Grunk!

Wanna disappeared among the cycads and pines. Jamie ran in after him and caught up just as the little dinosaur was gobbling down another gingko.

'I'm glad you don't get tired of your favourite food,' said Jamie. 'I'd never be able to follow Tom's trail on my own.'

They set off
between the dense
trunks, Wanna with his
snout to the ground.

BOOM! BOOM!

A deep, sinister sound
made them stop in their
tracks.

BOOM!
BOOM! BOOM!

The ground was
shaking under their feet.
The next instant a huge
dinosaur had burst out
into a clearing ahead.

It stomped heavily along on its two back legs, head whipping this way and that, its slavering jaws full of razor-sharp teeth.

Jamie steered Wanna to safety behind a broad-trunked tree.

'Don't move, boy,' he whispered. 'That's one massive monster–and it looks hungry.'

The towering dinosaur barged among the trees, raising its snout now and again as if it could smell something good to eat. Jamie could see it was a fighter–it had battle scars all over its body.

'Ferocious ten-metre long dino,'

he muttered to himself, 'bigger than an allosaurus, gigantic back legs, serrated teeth of a carnivore, bumps above the eyes. I may not have the Fossil Finder but I'm guessing that's a megalosaurus.' He gasped as the dinosaur avidly sniffed the air. 'We're in trouble, Wanna. It's a nasty predator and it's got our scent.'

The megalosaurus was slowly heading their way, flattening bushes and crunching branches as it approached. They could hear its heavy, snorting breath. Peeping through the leaves, Jamie could see its battered, scarred face.

I've only got a few seconds before it's got us, he thought.

His eyes swept the ground and fell upon a hairy, coconut-like fruit. Very slowly he bent and picked it up.

'No, Wanna,' he warned in a low voice as the eager little dino tried to take a bite of it. 'It's all we've got to distract the megalosaurus.'

Jamie wished Tom was here. Escaping from scary dinosaurs was much easier with a friend. But he

took a deep
breath and hurled
the furry ball as far as
he could manage,
but it only made
it to a tree trunk
a few metres away.

Jamie held his breath
as the megalosaurus swung its head
in the direction of the tree and took
two steps towards it. But after a few
sniffs, the beast turned back towards
Jamie and Wanna.

That almost worked, Jamie thought.
I've just got to throw it further away.

The dinosaur was just a few steps

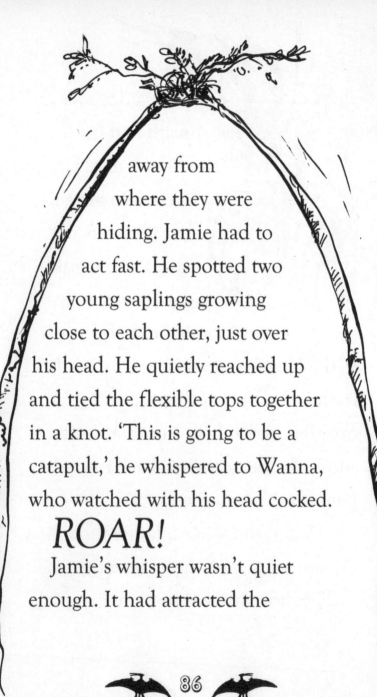

away from
where they were
hiding. Jamie had to
act fast. He spotted two
young saplings growing
close to each other, just over
his head. He quietly reached up
and tied the flexible tops together
in a knot. 'This is going to be a
catapult,' he whispered to Wanna,
who watched with his head cocked.

ROAR!

Jamie's whisper wasn't quiet
enough. It had attracted the

dinosaur's attention. Its beady eyes were fixed on their hiding place.

Jamie quickly placed the fruit at the top and bent the saplings back

as far as he could, straining with the effort.

'This had better work!' he muttered as he let go. The young trees whipped up, sending the

fruit sailing through the air, high
over the giant dino's head. It
crashed down through the
branches behind the
slavering creature.
Its sharp ears
picked up

the sound immediately.
It shot round with a
rumbling cry and set off
to follow it.

Jamie punched the air in
delight. 'It's sent him in the
opposite direction to where
we want to go. And we're not
going to be here when he comes
back. Find some more of Tom's
clues, Wanna.'

The little wannanosaurus
didn't need telling
twice. He galloped
off into the thick
undergrowth
of the valley,
nosing out the trail
of gingkoes. Jamie
followed, trying to
keep his eager friend in sight as he
scampered ahead following the path
of the river. He stopped to listen now
and again but there were no heavy
footsteps coming their way. At last
the trail led them away from the river
towards a sheer rock face.

Grunk!

Wanna snuffled about in search of more fruit.

Jamie's heart sank as he gazed up at the rock that towered above him. The gingko trail had led them to the mountains, but now they'd come to a dead end and Wanna didn't seem to be able to smell any more gingkoes. The pterosaurs could have taken Tom miles away by now, off to a high peak somewhere to be gobbled up between them. Jamie couldn't bear to think of such a thing happening to his friend.

He sat down despondently on a small boulder. Wanna trotted over to him and gently nudged his hand. He seemed to know that there was something wrong.

Jamie stroked the little dinosaur's head. 'You did your best, Wanna,' he told him. 'But I'm not sure what to do next.'

Then, to Jamie's surprise, Wanna suddenly trotted a little way off along the bottom of the cliff and began to make snuffling, slurping noises in the undergrowth.

'If I didn't know better I'd think you'd got another one of your favourite snacks!' said Jamie, going over to see what the little dinosaur had found. Wanna looked up-his snout was covered in gingko pulp!

Jamie gave a gasp of excitement. 'Brilliant, Wanna!' he yelled. 'You've sniffed out another clue. Tom must have come this way!'

High up in the pterosaur nest Tom was looking desperately round for an escape route. If he tried climbing down the rock face he'd certainly fall to his death. The nearest tree, whose top was higher than the nest, was well out of reach-too far away for Tom to risk a jump.

The gingkoes I dropped could have

Chip! Chip!

Chip! Chip!

been eaten straight *away*, he thought despairingly. And *without a trail to follow, Jamie and Wanna will never find me.*

In the distance the two pterosaurs were circling the valley. Any minute now they could be back for their human feast.

Chip! Chip!

One of the huge eggs in the nest
was moving and a crack ran across
its surface. The crack grew wider and
soon the tip of a beak could be seen
hacking away at the shell. At last a big
round eye appeared. For a moment

Tom forgot his plight
and watched, fascinated, as a
pterosaur chick emerged, covered
in slime and pieces of eggshell.
It wobbled on two spindly legs and
tried to shake the shell off its sticky
wings. It let out a high-pitched
squawk.

'Poor thing,' said Tom, picking
the shell from the chick's skin.
Every time it saw his hand moving it
opened its mouth hungrily. 'Don't

worry about food,' Tom told it
bitterly. 'You'll probably be nibbling
bits of me later.'

As if it had understood, the
chick poked its beak at his hand,
squawking loudly.

'Shhh!' said Tom, scanning the
skies. '*You* might want to see your
mum and dad, but *I* certainly don't!'

Then Tom heard another sound.
He tensed and listened hard. No, he
must have been imagining it.

'TOM!' It was Jamie's voice. Tom
looked around wildly. 'Tom, where
are you?'

Tom crawled to the edge of the

precipice and looked down. He couldn't believe his eyes.

Far below him were Jamie and Wanna. Jamie was waving and Wanna was trying in vain to climb the cliff.

'I'm so pleased to see you!' yelled Tom. 'I worried something would have eaten the trail of gingkoes.'

'Something did eat them,' Jamie yelled back. 'Guess who.'

Grunk!

'Good old Wanna!' shouted Tom. 'Now all I've got to do is get down from here. Any ideas?'

Jamie pulled some long vines from the massive tree growing closest to the rock face.

'I'm coming to get you,' he called.

He coiled the vines over his shoulder and began the difficult climb. The rough bark grazed his knees. Halfway up his foot slipped and he felt the branch crack below him. He shot out an arm and clung on to a knot in the trunk. He dangled desperately trying to get

a foothold. At last he wedged his
toes into the bark.

'Are you all right?' he heard Tom
shout in alarm.

'I'm OK!' he panted. 'Soon be
there.'

After what seemed an age, he
reached the top branches and poked
his head out to see Tom grinning at
him from the cliff ledge.

'Where's the backpack?' Jamie asked.

'I've got everything here,' Tom replied. 'Even the toffees! I know better than to leave anything in Dino World.'

They could hear faint *grunks* from the ground below.

'Wanna thinks we've abandoned him,' said Jamie.

'Don't worry, boy,' Tom called down to the anxious little dino. 'We'll be back soon.'

'Cool!' exclaimed Jamie, catching sight of the pterosaur chick who was squawking loudly from its nest.

'As soon as its parents hear that racket they'll be down to feed it,' warned Tom. 'And we'll be pterosaur tea.'

'I've got an escape plan.' Jamie scrambled further up the tree. He looped the vine rope over a branch and tied one end firmly round his waist. 'Get ready to catch the other end,' he called, swinging it over to Tom.

Tom caught it.

'Now jump,' instructed Jamie.

Tom looked down at the drop.

'I can't do it,' he said.

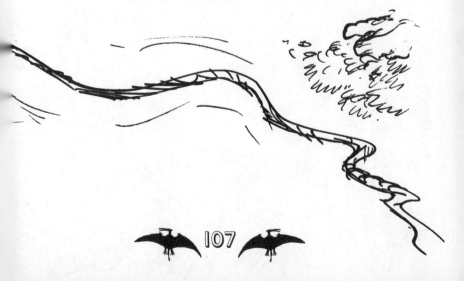

'There's no other way,' Jamie replied. 'You've got to jump.'

CAW!

The pterosaurs were back.

Tom jerked his head up. They were diving straight at them.

'You have to,' yelled Jamie. 'And right now!'

CHAPTER 8

Still clinging on to the vine tied
around Jamie's waist, Tom leapt
off the ledge just as the two flying
serpents dived in to attack. As he
crashed into the spikey branches,
he caught a flash of their huge, sharp
claws and heard their angry cries.
But he had made it to the tree.

The boys scurried down the tree

as quickly as they could, and as soon
as they reached the ground Wanna
grunked round them in delight.

'Thanks for that, Jamie,' said Tom.
'Any time you're stuck in a pterosaur
nest, waiting to be fed to its babies–I
owe you one!'

There was a sharp cry
overhead. Jamie looked
up. 'Well, you don't have
to wait long to repay me. The
pterosaurs haven't given up.'
'Run!' shouted Tom.
'Make for the thickest
trees. They won't be able
to get us there.'

They dashed away
down the valley, following
the river. The pterosaurs
screeched and swooped above the
forest, trying to find a way through.
All of a sudden the trees ahead
gave way to low undergrowth. And
beyond that–the open plains.

'They'll snatch us up easily if we go across there,' panted Jamie. 'There's no shelter. But we can't stay here for ever.'

'Fancy a swim?' Tom pointed towards the river. It rushed down, white foam tumbling against boulders and drifting tree branches. 'I saw it from the air. It goes off to the east but then it cuts back near the jungle. It'll be fast but we're good enough swimmers.'

'We'll be all right, but what about Wanna?' asked Jamie. 'He can't swim and we can't leave him to run along the bank. The pterosaurs will pick him off easily.'

'I've got it!' said Tom. 'We can make a boat for him, a sort of raft.' He began to gather some short fallen branches.

'Good idea,' said Jamie, helping him. 'We can tie them together with vines.'

'Better be quick though.' Tom peered up through the leaves. The angry pterosaurs were circling right overhead.

Jamie nodded. 'We'll only have time to make it big enough for Wanna–and my backpack. We'll hang on to the edge and make sure he stays low.'

They lashed the branches together tightly with lengths of creeper.

'That should be big enough,' said Tom, leaning back on his heels and gazing at their rough craft. 'Let's hope it's riverworthy.'

They lifted it up and moved to the edge of the trees.

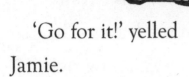

'Go for it!' yelled
Jamie.

Holding the raft over their heads
like a shield, they made a dash for
the riverbank, Wanna scuttling
underneath.

CAAAAW!

The pterosaurs dived towards
them. Jamie went tumbling as one
leathery wing caught him on the
back. Tom hauled him to his feet and
pulled him down the bank into the
cold, frothy water.

'Get on board,
Wanna,' he

shouted as they set it afloat and held
on tightly to stop it being taken off
by the strong current.

Wanna peered anxiously at the raft. Tom put the backpack on it and fixed the strap around the end of a log.

'You can do it, boy,' urged Jamie. The pterosaurs were wheeling round for another attack. 'The sooner we get back the sooner you can have a nice gingko treat.'

But the little wannanosaurus backed away. Suddenly there was a rush of air above him.

CAW!

A pterosaur was diving straight for his head.

Wanna took a running jump
and landed on the raft. It bobbed
and bucked but kept afloat. Wanna
immediately flattened himself in
terror.

Jamie and Tom pushed off into
the current and they sped along in
the rough water.

Their pursuers took to the sky,
heading back for their nest. Now the

danger was over, Wanna put his head up and grunked fiercely at them.

'That's right, Wanna,' laughed Tom. 'See them off! We're not such easy targets now we're moving so fast, and they've given up. We're safe at last.'

'Not yet!' Jamie yelled back.

The raft was nearly snatched from their hands. It spun and twisted, taking all their strength to keep a grip.

GRUNK!

'We've hit rapids,' spluttered Jamie. 'Hold on tight.'

The raft thudded against rock after rock and shot down mini waterfalls of foam. The boys felt themselves tumbling helplessly in the current but they kept their hands clamped to the raft, knuckles white with the strain. Wanna watched everything silently.

After three little waterfalls and one bend, at last the river grew calmer.

'Wow!' gasped Tom. 'That was exciting. Though I feel a bit battered.'

'I've got bruises on my bruises,' laughed Jamie, looking over his shoulder.

'We've reached the plains,' said Jamie, looking over at the bank.

'And after a while the river will bend back towards the jungle,' said Tom.

They let themselves be carried gently along, through the flat, dry landscape.

'We've seen no sign of any people,' said Jamie.

'And I've had an aerial view,' agreed Tom. 'Your dad must have been right. There must be another explanation for that professor's find.'

At last a wide curve of the river carried them into a swampy area. They grabbed a trailing root and pulled their makeshift raft over to the bank. The hills rose ahead, covered in the dark green of the trees. A short climb and they'd be back at the cave.

They climbed out, helped Wanna off his little boat, and began to make their way across the soft, muddy ground.

Tom took out his compass. 'I reckon we need to go due west to get to Gingko Cave.'

'Sounds good to me,' said Jamie.

'Come on, Wanna.'

They picked their way across the
steamy swamp towards the hills that
rose up in front of them. Their trainers
squelched in the deep mud as they
tried to find patches of firm ground.

The sky was full of grey stormy
clouds now and a fine rain began
to fall.

'What's that?' gasped Jamie suddenly, pointing ahead at a strange mound he could just make out through the misty air.

'It's a dead dino,' said Tom as they got closer. 'Looks like a brachiosaurus.'

They walked round the gigantic body, which lay between them and the trees. Wanna hung back, sniffing the air anxiously.

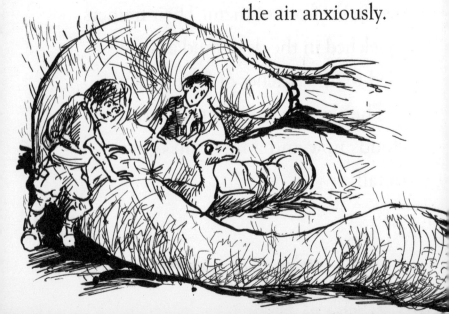

'Wow!' exclaimed Tom, touching the scaly skin. 'It's so huge.'

Grunk!

Wanna nudged at them as if he was getting them to move away.

'Wanna seems scared,' said Jamie. 'It can't hurt you, boy,' he told the little dinosaur.

At that moment they heard a deep, thunderous roar. They whirled round to see a herd of massive dinosaurs splashing across the swamp. The largest raised his head and roared again.

'Uh oh,' said Tom in a low voice. 'So that's what Wanna was trying to tell us.'

'Megalosaurs,' muttered Jamie. 'We're in trouble.'

CHAPTER 9

SEARCH:

'Hide!' hissed Tom.

The boys dived behind a nearby conifer.

Trembling, Wanna pushed in between them. They crouched in their hiding place, watching through the spiky branches as the huge dinosaurs made for the brachiosaurus's body. The rain was

falling steadily now, making swirling puddles of mud and splashing all about the carcass. With hungry roars, the massive creatures began to tear into the flesh.

'We'd better sit it out until they've gone,' whispered Jamie. 'We can't

risk being seen.' He looked up at the steep slope behind him. 'That's the way home but they'd be sure to spot us scrambling up there.'

Tom held an imaginary microphone to his mouth.

'And here we have the magnificent megalosaurs,' he whispered. 'These towering predators have found an easy meal here in the swamp. The meggies are having a tasty brachiosaurus dinner.'

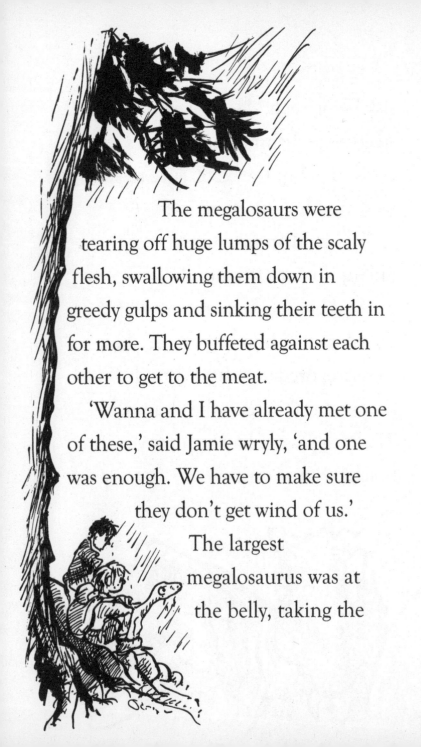

The megalosaurs were tearing off huge lumps of the scaly flesh, swallowing them down in greedy gulps and sinking their teeth in for more. They buffeted against each other to get to the meat.

'Wanna and I have already met one of these,' said Jamie wryly, 'and one was enough. We have to make sure they don't get wind of us.'

The largest megalosaurus was at the belly, taking the

biggest share of the food. If any of others came near, he warned them off with deep rumbling growls. The others backed away nervously.

'That must be the leader,' whispered Tom. 'He certainly seems to be in charge.'

They watched as the leader ate his fill. The rain was getting heavier and the sky had grown dark and stormy.

'Perhaps this is a good time to make a move,' said Jamie, trying to stop the drips going down his neck. 'They may not see us now the light's so bad.' Then he noticed something moving through the swamp. 'What's

that?' he whispered.
'It's another
megalosaurus,'
said Tom.

Now Jamie
could see
burning yellow
eyes and a
familiar battered face.
'Old Scarface,' he
told Tom. 'That's the
one Wanna and I had a close
shave with before we found
you. He can't be part of this herd or
he'd have been with them when they
arrived to eat.'

With a tremendous roar, the
newcomer lurched towards the herd,
whipping his head round on its
powerful neck. He stared hungrily at
the brachiosaurus meat, his mouth
drooling.

Grunk!

Wanna seemed to remember
the fierce dino from their earlier
encounter. He turned to run away,
his paws scrabbling on the muddy
slope.

'No, Wanna,' hissed Tom,
grabbing a front leg and
holding him firmly. 'It's too
dangerous. Stay still.'

Scarface pounded towards the corpse.

'He's determined not to miss out on dinner,' said Jamie.

The head of the herd had raised his bloodstained snout to look at the interloper. He gave an answering roar, raised himself to his full height, and snapped his jaws. Scarface bared his sharp teeth, thumping his tail hard on the ground.

The megalosaurs circled each other, heads high, snarling horribly.

'The leader's not going to let him get at their food,' said Tom. 'He sees this as a leadership challenge.'

'He's going to fight Scarface,' agreed Jamie. 'And that means a fight to the death.'

The rain was hammering down now, splattering the two megalosaurs as they stalked angrily around each other. The other dinosaurs moved back to get out of the way of the fight.

'I've seen this sort of thing on television with animals today,' whispered Jamie. 'The herd follows the winner. They're impressed by his strength and too scared to disobey.'

Scarface made the first move,

slashing at the leader with his fierce
front claws.

His opponent gave an angry roar
as three bleeding slashes appeared on
his neck. He swung his tail round,
thumping into Scarface and sending
him staggering back. The other
megalosaurs grunted and stamped
their feet.

'Scarface won't give up that easily,'
whispered Jamie. 'He's a mean
customer.'

Jamie was right. The newcomer suddenly lunged forwards, catching the leader by surprise and butting him hard in the chest. The leader retaliated by grabbing him with his front legs and biting down hard on his shoulder.

'Scarface looks badly injured,' said Tom. 'That gash is bleeding heavily.'

'He's still fighting though,' gasped Jamie as the battle-marked dino launched himself again at the leader, churning up the red mud.

They locked together in a frenzy of claws and teeth. With an angry bellow the leader threw Scarface off,

making him reel back. He
crashed into the tree where
the boys and Wanna were hiding.
Then he shook himself and launched
himself back down into the swamp,
making for his enemy.

'That was close!' gasped Jamie.

CREAK!

They looked up to where the ominous noise was coming from. The trunk of the damaged conifer was splitting, throwing splinters of bark into the air.

Wanna gave an anxious grunk.

'Uh-oh!' cried Tom.
'That tree's coming
down.'
  'It's going to fall
on us!' yelled Jamie.
'Move!'

CHAPTER 10

Jamie, Tom, and Wanna dived out of the way as the thick tree trunk crashed to the ground. Tom cried out as a branch hit his face.

'Are you OK?' asked Jamie anxiously as they cowered next to the fallen conifer. Sticky yellow resin was leaking out from the trunk and oozing down to the ground.

Tom wiped his mouth and found a smear of blood on his hand. 'That hit me right in the jaw,' he answered, rubbing his jaw. 'It's not too bad but . . . oh!'

'What?' Jamie asked, sensing his friend's panic.

'Oh no!' Tom gasped and suddenly dived among the branches of the fallen trunk.

'What are you doing?' asked Jamie.

'That branch knocked out my loose tooth,' explained Tom. 'It's fallen out somewhere and I've got to get it back.'

'Leave it,' said Jamie urgently.

Tom turned to his friend, his fingers covered in the sticky resin. 'I can't,' he told him. 'I've just had a horrible thought. If my tooth has fallen in this stuff, it will become trapped in amber in millions of years' time. And you know what that means.'

Jamie gulped. 'That will be the tooth that the professor found in our time. He'll use it as proof that there *were* people around in the Jurassic era.'

'It will mess up all the dino timelines and everything,' Tom finished.

A huge megalosaurus foot stamped down on the branches by their heads.

The two dinosaurs were still battling for leadership. Wanna grunked in alarm as he followed the boys up the slope to hide in some bushes.

'We'll have to leave the tooth,' panted Jamie. 'We've got no choice. I'd rather leave a tooth behind than have the fossilized hand we saw to be from one of us!'

The rain was a torrent now, causing rivulets to rush down the slope. The water carried soil and leaves from the higher ground, adding to the mud. They could hear distant thunder.

Heads down, the boys and Wanna clawed their way up the slope away

from the roaring dinosaurs and the watching herd.

They suddenly stopped and froze. Through the driving rain they could see two megalosaurs in their path–a mother and her baby.

The mother had her eyes fixed on the fight. Her baby, no bigger than Wanna, watched from behind a cycad tree, its eyes big and round with fright.

'They haven't seen us,' said Jamie, as the boys and Wanna edged sideways to avoid them.

'We'll have to take the long way round.' Tom scoured the hills.

There was a
rumbling sound
on the slope above
and all of a sudden
a wall of mud
came surging
down towards the two
dinosaurs, sweeping up
trees and boulders in
its path.

'Landslide!'
cried Jamie.

At the sight of the approaching mud slick the mother megalosaurus gave a frightened roar and bolted off towards the swamp.

Grabbing Wanna between them, the boys threw themselves clear of the deadly avalanche of earth. When they looked round they could see that a deep mound of mud had built up around the cycad. The baby was

trapped up to its neck in the middle of it. It was making terrified calls

and shaking its head desperately.
At last it pulled one front leg free
but that seemed to have exhausted
it and it sank its head down on the
sodden earth.

'We've got to do something,' said Jamie. 'We can't just leave it.'

The baby megalosaurus was writhing helplessly, trying to free itself as it sank further into the earth.

'It's calling for its mother again,' said Jamie. 'But she's too far away to hear.'

'It's up to us to free it then,' declared Tom. 'But without being seen. The minute any adult megalosaurs spot us we're dead meat.'

'Even the baby could attack us,' warned Jamie. 'We've never had to get a carnivore out of trouble before. We don't know how it'll react. But we've got no choice.'

He peered through the driving
rain. Down below in the swamp, the
herd had their eyes fixed on their
leader and Scarface who were still
battling away.

Followed closely by Wanna, the
boys waded into the thick mud of the
landslide.

Tom slipped and fell, pulling Jamie

with him. The mud sucked at their hands and feet as they tried to get up. At last, caked in earth and wet through, they struggled to their feet and clawed their way towards the baby. Wanna scrambled after them, trembling with fear at every roar of the gigantic beasts below.

Above the fury of the fight there was a flash of light and a deafening crash of thunder.

'The storm's overhead,' cried Tom. 'There's sure to be more landslides with all this heavy rain.'

'We've got to save the baby meggie now,' shouted Jamie.

They had
almost reached the
stranded baby when
one of the megalosaurs
whipped round, alerted
by their movement. It
let out a roar that sent vibrations
through them.

The cry roused
the rest of the herd.
Heads turned, teeth
flashed, and an
army of massive
legs started
moving up the
slope towards the
boys.

'Got to get
away,' panted
Tom, tugging

at Jamie's arm as the terrifying megalosaurs surged towards them.

'We'll never move fast enough through this mud,' gasped Jamie.

The huge carnivores barged and snapped at each other, each one eager to be the first to get to its prey.

Jamie, Tom, and Wanna shrank away from the slavering jaws. They were trapped. Nothing could save them from these terrible monsters now.

CHAPTER 11

SEARCH:

Suddenly above their heads there
was a tremendous rumbling, as if an
underground train was going to burst
out from the hillside.

The rumbling grew louder and
now Jamie and Tom could feel
vibrations running through their feet
and up their legs.

The megalosaurs stopped in their deadly approach.

Grunk!

Wanna's eyes were wide with terror.

'Look out!' yelled Jamie, pushing the little dinosaur out of the way as a huge rock came bouncing down the side of the hill.

The megalosaurs gave petrified roars and stampeded away.

The baby squealed in panic, rocking its head from side to side and feebly waving its front leg.

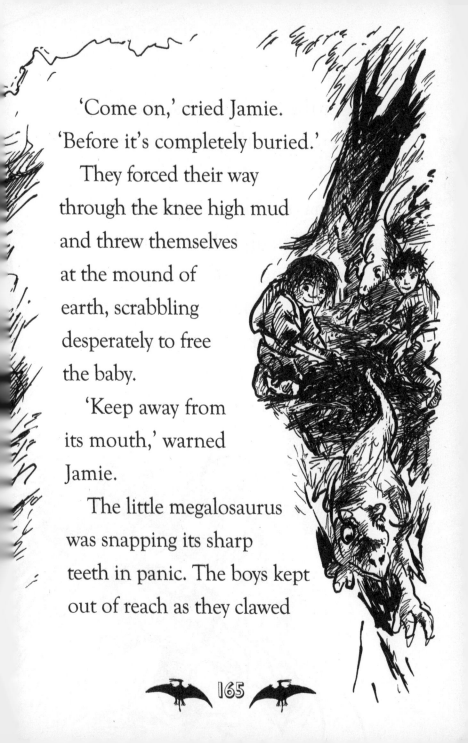

'Come on,' cried Jamie.
'Before it's completely buried.'

They forced their way
through the knee high mud
and threw themselves
at the mound of
earth, scrabbling
desperately to free
the baby.

'Keep away from
its mouth,' warned
Jamie.

The little megalosaurus
was snapping its sharp
teeth in panic. The boys kept
out of reach as they clawed

at its earthy prison. At last they had
uncovered the other front leg.

Grunk!

Wanna dug like a dog sending the
mud spraying up behind him.

'It's working,' yelled Tom.

With a tremendous wriggle the
baby broke free and bolted
down the slope, crying for
its mother.

'Brilliant!' exclaimed Jamie. 'We did it!'

'Time to get out of here,' shouted Tom. 'That scientist might have found my tooth but that's all he's going to find.'

There was a blinding flash of lightning followed by a rumble of thunder. But instead of dying away, the rumble seemed to be getting louder.

Jamie looked up, dashing the driving rain from his eyes.

'We've got to go NOW!' he bellowed. 'The whole side of the hill is coming down.'

They scrambled and slipped sideways out of the path, Wanna darting ahead, using all four feet to escape.

CRASH!

They were just in time. An avalanche of mud and boulders tumbled down, completely engulfing where they'd been standing.

Tom and Jamie stood panting in the pelting rain.

'I'm glad we're not under that!' gasped Tom.

There was a crackle
of breaking branches and
suddenly a megalosaurus
head poked out of the
bushes nearby.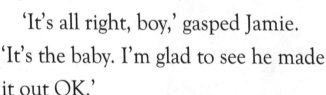

Grunk!

Wanna gave a warning
cry.

'It's all right, boy,' gasped Jamie.
'It's the baby. I'm glad to see he made
it out OK.'

The little megalosaurus made a
small cry in its throat.

'He's saying thank you,' said Tom.
He gave a bow. 'Not at all, youngster.
It was our pleasure.'

'Just promise not to eat us if we meet again,' added Jamie.

'I don't think it works like that,' said Tom with a laugh.

The baby gazed solemnly at them for a moment then turned and trundled off through the trees to find its mother.

'Race you back to the cave,' said Tom with a grin. 'We need to see that TV update and find out if they've discovered

anything more about the tooth. I
hope it was mine. Then we'll know
there haven't been any other humans
here.'

'Though I want to hear what
they think about that hand,' replied
Jamie. He burst out laughing. 'Can
you imagine if they found a fossilized
Fossil Finder!'

Wanna bounded ahead as the boys
sprinted through the jungle and up
the hill to Gingko Cave. Tom went
over to a gingko tree and picked a
handful of fruit.

'Here you are, boy,' he said,
putting them on the ground and

patting Wanna on his hard, domed head. 'This is a thank you for leading Jamie to the rescue.'

The little dinosaur settled down happily with his juicy snack.

The boys walked backwards in the footprints and soon found themselves in the smugglers' cave in Dinosaur Cove. As they made their way across the cave floor, the mud stains on their clothes and skin turned to dust.

'I wonder if the tooth fairy knows the way to Dino World,' said Tom with a grin. He prodded at the gap in

his mouth with his tongue.

'You could always leave her a map under your pillow!' said Jamie. 'Though she'll have a job. It'll be like looking for a pilchard in the ocean as Grandad always says.'

They stepped out into the sunshine and Jamie looked at their clothes.

'We can't go home like this,' he said. 'We're covered in Jurassic dust!'

'A quick dip in the sea first
then,' suggested Tom. The boys
scrambled down over the
rocks, sneaked across the
beach and plunged into the

sea to wash themselves clean. Then
they sprinted up to the lighthouse
and burst into Dad's office just as the
newsflash was starting.

The reporter was outside the cave
again.

'We come back to you with breaking
news,' he told the camera. 'Experts

have examined the tooth and agreed
it is indeed human. It's a milk tooth,
probably from a child of about nine.'

'I don't believe it!' gasped Dad.
'There can't have been humans in
the Jurassic age.'

Jamie and Tom tried not to look at
each other.

'I have Professor Jenkins here with me now,' the reporter went on. The camera swung to show the scientist, rocking on his heels and looking very pleased with himself. 'There's a bit more to the report, Professor. Perhaps you could explain what it means to our viewers.'

The scientist looked puzzled.

'The fossilized hand has also been examined,' said the reporter coldly. 'It's a fake! What have you got to say about that?'

'Well . . . it's . . . ' the professor spluttered.

'It's made up of the bones from a gibbon and an orang-utan,' said the reporter. 'And it's only about forty years old. And as for the tooth. It might be real and I'm told that the amber round it certainly was very old but the experts are working on how you pulled off that stunt.' He turned back to the screen. 'So there you have it. There were no humans alive two hundred and fifty million years ago. I'm afraid this will go down in history as the Bogus Bones of Bridwell Bay.'

Professor Jenkins was bright red in the face. 'OK, I admit it; I made up the hand fossil,' he blustered. 'But the tooth's genuine. It really is. I found it right here, in amber in the rock.'

'If the tooth's genuine,' snapped the reporter, 'how do you explain the traces of toffee found on it. Are you saying there were sweet shops back in the Jurassic?'

Jamie and Tom burst out laughing.
Dad switched the TV off.

'What a fool that man was,' he
said. 'Can you imagine it–humans
in the world of the dinosaurs!
Impossible.'

Jamie and Tom looked at each other
and grinned. Only they knew how
'impossible' it really was!

DINOSAUR WORLD

- - - - BOYS' ROUTE

✗ WHERE TOM IS SNATCHED BY PTEROSAURS

Humongous Waterfall

Massive Canyon

Plains

Fin Rock ◁

Jurassic Ocean

GLOSSARY

Allosaurus (al-oh-sor-us) – one of the largest meat-eating dinosaurs and one of the fiercest predators of its time. Its name means 'different lizard' because its backbone was shaped differently than other dinosaurs.

Archaeopteryx (ar-kee-op-ter-ix) – small bird-like feathered creature, capable of flight. It had sharp teeth, three clawed fingers, a long bony tail, and a second toe for use as a 'killing claw'. Archaeopteryx was not a fussy feeder, eating small animals, plants, and insects.

Brachiosaurus (bra-kee-oh-sor-us) – had a long neck, like a giraffe. This gentle giant loved its greens, munching through around 150 kgs of plants a day!

Camarasaurus (cam-ah–roh-sor-us) – a long-necked, long-tailed giant herbivore with spoon-shaped teeth and a hollow backbone.

Cretaceous (cret-ay-shus) – from about 65 to 150 million years ago, this time period was home to the widest variety of dinosaur and insect life of any period. Birds replaced winged dinosaurs, while in the sea, sharks and rays multiplied.

Cycads (si-kads) – plants with thick trunks, palm-like leaves, and cones.

Diplodocus (dip-lod-oh-kus) – one of the longest land dinosaurs with a long-neck and whip-like tail. This huge dinosaur had pencil-shaped blunt teeth perfect for its plant-only diet.

Gingko (gink-oh) – a tree native to China called a 'living fossil' because fossils of it have been found dating back millions of years, yet they are still around today. Also known as the stink bomb tree because of its smelly apricot-like fruit.

Jurassic (jur-as-sick) – from about 150 to 200 million years ago, the Jurassic age was warm and humid, with lush jungle cover and great marine diversity. Large dinosaurs ruled on land, while the first birds took to the air.

Megalosaurus (meg-ah-loh-sor-us) – a large meat-eating dinosaur of the Jurassic Period. It was the first dinosaur to be discovered and named.

Pterosaur (ter-oh-sor) – a prehistoric flying reptile. Its wings were leathery and light and some of these 'winged lizards' had fur on their bodies and bony crests on their heads.

Stegosaurus (steg-oh-sor-us) – a large plant-eating dinosaur. It had heavy plated armour and a long row of kite shaped spikes down its spine, and another row behind its shoulders for defence.

Wannanosaurus (wah-nan-oh-sor-us) – a dinosaur that only ate plants and used its hard, flat skull to defend itself. Named after the place it was discovered: Wannano in China.

CONTINUE YOUR
JURASSIC ADVENTURE...

CONTINUE YOUR
JURASSIC ADVENTURE...

EXPLORE CREATE DISCOVER PLAY

Dinosaur Cove
REXSTONE™

Bursting with awesome dino-facts, puzzles and activities!

JURASSIC SURVIVAL GUIDE

Want to join Jamie and Tom's gang?

HAVE HOURS OF FUN
WITH COOL DINO GAMES?

GET EXCLUSIVE
BONUS CONTENT?

ENTER GREAT COMPETITIONS
TO WIN AWESOME PRIZES?

FIND OUT EVEN MORE
AMAZING DINO FACTS?

Then get ready for the best fun EVER as you enter the world of

Dinosaur Cove™

www.dinosaurcove.co.uk

(Just watch out for the t-rex!)